The Saracen Maid

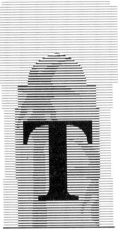

THE
FRIENDS
of the
Beverly Hills
Public Library

$\int$ The
aracen $\mathcal{M}$ aid

by Leon Garfield
illustrated by John O'Brien

SIMON & SCHUSTER BOOKS FOR YOUNG READERS
Published by Simon & Schuster
New York London Toronto Sydney Tokyo Singapore

SIMON & SCHUSTER BOOKS FOR YOUNG READERS
1230 Avenue of the Americas, New York, New York 10020
Text copyright © 1991 by Leon Garfield
Illustrations copyright © 1994 by John O'Brien
First published in Great Britain in 1991 by Simon
& Schuster Young Books. First U.S. Edition 1994
SIMON & SCHUSTER BOOKS FOR YOUNG READERS
is a trademark of Simon & Schuster.
The text of this book is set in 16-point Sabon.
The illustrations were done in watercolor.
Manufactured in the United States of America

10   9   8   7   6   5   4   3   2   1

Library of Congress Cataloging-in-Publication Data
Garfield, Leon. The Saracen maid / Leon Garfield ;
illustrated by John O'Brien.   p.   cm.   Summary: After being
captured by pirates and sold as a slave, a forgetful young
Englishman faces a long imprisonment because he can't
remember where the ransom note should be sent.
[1. Memory — Fiction.   2. Adventure and adventurers — Fiction.
3. Humorous stories.]   I. O'Brien, John, ill.   II. Title.
PZ7.G17943Sar   1994 [Fic] — dc20   93–6612 CIP
ISBN: 0–671–86646–X

Contents

1. Don't Forget Your Head!

One April morning long, long ago,
in the year eleven hundred and something
or other, when London was like a garden
with a wall all around, a wall so high that
three good-sized Londoners standing on
one another's shoulders could only just reach
up to rescue a cat, a certain young man
in a crimson cloak and yellow stockings,
like plums and custard, was getting ready
to go to sea.

Gilbert Becket was his name — that is, when he didn't forget it.

"You'd forget your head, young Gilbert," said his father, who had a house in Cheapside and a prosperous business in the silk and woollen trade, "if it wasn't held down by your hat!" But of course, as his head was the part he forgot with, it would really have been the other way around.

But it was April already and high time for setting out to buy goods from the East. It was Gilbert's turn to go.

"Have you remembered what you are going for, young Gilbert?" his father asked.

"Of course, Father! I'm going to buy silks and dyes for the trade."

"Well done, my boy!"

"And have you remembered where you are going, young Gilbert?" asked his mother, with a sigh and a shake of her head.

"Of course, Mother! I'm going to the land of flying carpets, where people wear baggy trousers and cork up demons in bottles! I'm going to the East!"

"Well done, my son!"

Nevertheless, everybody went down to the river, where the sailors were singing and swarming and swinging in a forest of masts, just to make sure that Gilbert got on the right ship.

"Don't forget us, young Gilbert!" they cried as he stepped aboard. "Fare you well, and remember to come back home!"

The sailors cast off and the ship moved away, leaving a garden of waving hats and handkerchiefs and tears as bright as the dew.

"Yo! Heave ho!" sang the sailors as they sailed downriver. Then they changed their tune to a hymn for good weather as London vanished and England slipped away into mists.

2. Barbary Pirates

They sailed by the sun, they sailed by the stars, first to Holland then along the edge of France. They sailed all the way around the corners of Spain. They turned east toward the port of Tyre, and sailed along the coast of North Africa.

The days were calm, the nights were warm, and the wind continued fair. But in every man's heart, though no man spoke it, was a secret fear.

Then early one morning a dark speck appeared, just where the sun rose dripping from the golden sea.

It grew and grew until it was a coal-black ship with a blood-red sail, and every man knew that his fear had come true!

"Pirates!" cried the helmsman. "Barbary pirates!" He fell to the deck with an arrow shot clean through his heart!

Then with a terrible shout and a flash of

swords, the pirates leaped aboard, and everyone was seized and put in chains, to be sold as slaves in Tyre.

Some went for silver, some went for gold, and some for as little as a jug of wine; but young Gilbert fetched the highest price of all. With his crimson cloak and good yellow stockings, he was plainly a rich man's son. He was bought by a baggy-trousered merchant with a mouth like a gash and eyes like a pair of stones.

3. Bread and Water

"There's sure to be somebody he's left at home who loves him enough to send me his weight in gold for his safe return!" said the merchant, in Arabic, to his daughter.

"Even twice his weight wouldn't be too much to ask!" said the merchant's clever daughter, a lovely Saracen maid, for she could see that young Gilbert was as slim as a flute.

"Who is your father and where does he live?" asked the merchant, making ready to write for the money. But alas! Gilbert was so frightened that he'd completely forgotten his father's name and the name of the street where he lived.

The merchant's brow grew dark with anger. He'd paid a high price for Gilbert, and now it looked as though he'd made a bad bargain and would be laughed at by all his friends. He cast young Gilbert into the dungeon and chained him to the wall.

"Stay there!" he shouted, with a shake of his fist. "You'll have nothing but bread and water until you remember who's going to pay for sending you home!"

But Gilbert couldn't remember. So for day after day and week after week, it was bread and water and a bed of straw. He would have wasted away until he was as light as a feather, if it hadn't been for the Saracen maid.

Secretly by night she brought him sherbet and pastries of almonds and pomegranate that

she'd made with her own hands. She knew
that if he got thinner, he wouldn't be worth
anything at all. Besides, she pitied him with all
her heart.

She begged him, in Arabic, to try to
remember; but he told her, in English, that
"Gilbert" and "London" were the best he
could do.

Then she sighed, and he sighed. That was a language they could both understand. The Saracen maid had fallen in love with Gilbert, and Gilbert, with his mouth full of pastry, loved her.

"Here!" she whispered, in Arabic. "Here is the key to your chains, and here is the key to the door. And here is some gold to get you back home. Don't forget me, because I'll always remember you. Fare you well, Gilbert, London, my love!"

4. A Week of Tears

Next morning there was a shouting and banging of fists on tables when the merchant found out that his prisoner had gone. And it was worse when his friends all came to laugh and tell him he should have locked up his daughter instead.

So he did. He locked her up in her bedroom as a punishment for what she'd done.

But the Saracen maid, after a week of tears, made up her mind to escape. First she sat on her carpet and commanded "London!" Alas! her father must have told it not to fly.

Then she opened a bottle and ordered
"Take me to Gilbert!" Alas! her father must
have put the demon to sleep.

So she made a rope of her sheets, for her father had forgotten she wasn't sleeping on straw, and climbed down from her window in the middle of the night, with as many of her jewels as she could carry.

She went down to the harbor and cried, "London! London!" to every ship's captain she met. At last she found one who knew where it was and was willing to take her for a ruby ring and diamond brooch.

So she sailed on the ship along the edge of Egypt, and then around the corners of Spain. She sailed along France until she reached Holland, and then turned north into the mists.

5. "Gilbert! Gilbert!"

*I*t was April when the ship reached London. A whole year had passed. She gazed up at the high wall that encircled the town, and said to herself, "My Gilbert is somewhere inside."

She left the ship and entered the town, crying "Gilbert! Gilbert!" in every street. Heads poked out of windows, boys turned around to stare, and even the horses shook their heads in wonderment as the Saracen maid passed by.

23

At last she came to Cheapside. Her sandals were worn out and her eyes were full of tears. Her voice was hoarse and she could hardly be heard as she cried out "Gilbert! Gilbert!"

"What's that?" asked young Gilbert, sitting at dinner in his father's house. "I thought I heard a voice calling out my name!"

His mother went to the window and said, "Why! It's a Saracen maid!"

"A Saracen maid?" said Gilbert, scratching his head. "Do I know a Saracen maid?" Then

he went downstairs and out into the street and straight into the arms of the Saracen maid!

"Gilbert!" She wept. "O my love!" cried he. "My wonderful Saracen maid!" Though she'd gone clean out of his head, for that was the part he forgot with, she'd stayed in his heart, for that was where he always remembered!

Great was the rejoicing in Cheapside, and the next day young Gilbert was married to the Saracen maid.

They lived long and happily together in the silk and woollen trade. They had a daughter called Agnes and a son called Thomas, who became a saint.